Every child learns to read in a different way and at his or her own speed. Some go back and forth between reading levels and read their favorite books again and again. Others read through each level in order. You can help your young reader improve and become more confident by encouraging his or her own interests and abilities. From books your child reads with you to the first books he or she reads alone, there are I Can Read Books for every stage of reading:

SHARED READING
Basic language, word repetition, and whimsical illustrations, ideal for sharing with your emergent reader

BEGINNING READING
Short sentences, familiar words, and simple concepts for children eager to read on their own

READING WITH HELP
Engaging stories, longer sentences, and language play for developing readers

READING ALONE
Complex plots, challenging vocabulary, and high-interest topics for the independent reader

I Can Read Books have introduced children to the joy of reading since 1957. Featuring award-winning authors and illustrators and a fabulous cast of beloved characters, I Can Read Books set the standard for beginning readers.

A lifetime of discovery begins with the magical words **"I Can Read!"**

Visit www.icanread.com for info
on enriching your child's reading e

D1385190

To our amazing editor, Virginia Duncan,
who has believed in this science series
from the very beginning
—K. D. & S. R. J.

For my big sister Mimi—
Thank you for everything!
—J. M.

The full-color artwork was created digitally.

I Can Read® and I Can Read Book® are trademarks of HarperCollins Publishers.

Library of Congress Control Number: 2023945925
ISBN 978-0-06-311663-4 (hardcover) — ISBN 978-0-06-311662-7 (paperback)

24 25 26 27 28 COS 10 9 8 7 6 5 4 3 2 1 ❖ First Edition
🎨 Greenwillow Books

Libby

LOVES SCIENCE

States of Matter

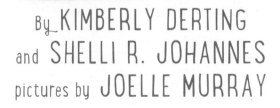

By KIMBERLY DERTING
and SHELLI R. JOHANNES
pictures by JOELLE MURRAY

Greenwillow Books
An Imprint of HarperCollins Publishers

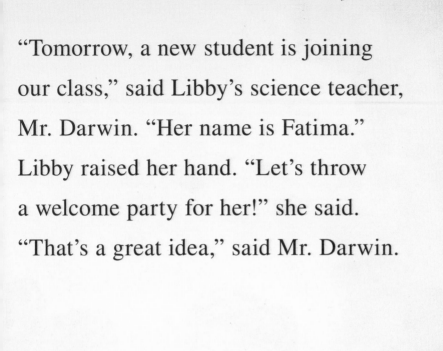

"Tomorrow, a new student is joining
our class," said Libby's science teacher,
Mr. Darwin. "Her name is Fatima."
Libby raised her hand. "Let's throw
a welcome party for her!" she said.
"That's a great idea," said Mr. Darwin.

Libby and her friends were excited to
meet Fatima.

"I can make a welcome sign," said Finn.

"I can get decorations," Rosa said.

"I can bring ingredients for ice cream sundaes," said Libby.

The next morning, Libby grabbed sprinkles, gummy bears, cookies, and marshmallows from the kitchen cabinet.
She packed up whipped cream, ice cream, and chocolate chips.

Libby's mother drove her to school.

"Don't forget to put the ice cream in
the freezer," Libby's mother said.

"I won't!" Libby jumped out of the car.
"Bye, Mom!"

Libby raced into school with a bag full
of fun ingredients. She couldn't wait!

Libby and her friends decorated the classroom for the welcome party.

They hung up the sign.

They strung the streamers.

Libby put her bag on the floor and set out
all the sundae toppings on the table.

The new student arrived just after the bell rang.

"Everyone, this is Fatima," said Mr. Darwin.

"Hi, Fatima!" they all said together.

Fatima smiled and sat down next to Libby.

"Is it time for the party?" Finn asked.

"Why don't we do some science first?"

said Mr. Darwin.

"I love science!" Fatima said.

"Me too!" Libby said. "Science is the best!"

"Today, we will learn about the different states of matter," Mr. Darwin said. "Matter is anything that takes up space and has mass." Mr. Darwin pointed to the board. "There are three states of matter: solid, liquid, and gas."

"My dog has gas," Finn said.

Everyone laughed, even Mr. Darwin.

Mr. Darwin got some ice from the freezer. "Let's start with solids," he said. "A solid is something that keeps its shape, such as this ice."

"Or that microscope," said Libby, pointing.

"Or a pencil," Rosa said, holding hers up.

"Or my chair," said Fatima.

Finn raised his hand. "Does that mean that everything in the classroom is a solid?" "Yes, except for anything that is a liquid or a gas," Mr. Darwin explained.

Mr. Darwin filled a glass with water.
"A liquid is anything that flows freely and doesn't have a shape," he said. "So it takes the shape of its container. See how this water is now the shape of the glass? Water is a liquid."

"Is milk a liquid?"
Rosa asked.

"Is juice?"
Fatima asked.

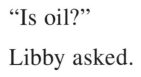

"Is oil?"
Libby asked.

"Yes. Those are all liquids,
too," said Mr. Darwin.

19

"Next, let's talk about gas," said Mr. Darwin.
"Remember, liquids flow freely and take
the shape of a container. A gas also has no
shape and flows freely, but unlike a liquid,
it expands to fill all of the container it is in."
Mr. Darwin held up a jar. "You can't see it,
but this jar is full of air."

"That means oxygen is a gas!" Fatima said.

"Right," said Mr. Darwin.

"And nitrogen!" said Finn.

"Right again," said Mr. Darwin. "Air is mainly made up of nitrogen and oxygen."

"The three states of matter are amazing!" said Libby.

"Does anyone have any questions?"
Mr. Darwin asked.

Fatima raised her hand. "Is there anything
that can be all three states at different times?"

"Great question!" said Mr. Darwin. "Any
guesses?"

"I know!" Libby exclaimed. "Water. It can be ice, water, and steam."

"You got it!" Mr. Darwin checked the clock. "Before we go to recess, what are the three states of matter called again?" he said.

"Solid, liquid, and gas," the class said together.

"Is everyone ready for Fatima's welcome party?" Mr. Darwin asked after recess. "Yes!" Libby and her friends yelled.

"I'm definitely ready for ice cream sundaes,"
Finn said.

"Me too!" said Libby. She went to get the ice
cream out of the bag on the floor.

Libby opened the container and saw the ice cream had melted.

"Oh, no!" Libby said. "I forgot to put the ice cream in the freezer."

Rosa looked at the milky mess. "It was a solid, but that is definitely a liquid now." "What will we have as a special treat?" Finn asked.

"Mr. Darwin, do you have anything else we can use?" asked Libby.

"I have hot chocolate mix," said Mr. Darwin.

"Yum! That's perfect," Libby said.

Mr. Darwin made hot chocolate for everyone.

Libby pointed at the steam coming from her mug. "Hey, this steam is a gas!" Mr. Darwin nodded. "That's right."

Rosa dumped marshmallows into her cup. "These are solids," she said.

Finn looked into his mug. "And this cocoa is a liquid."

"Those are the three states of matter," Fatima said. "Solids, liquids, and gases are everywhere."

31

"Look!" Rosa said. "My marshmallows are melting."

"They are turning into a liquid," said Fatima. That gave Libby an idea. "What if we cool down the hot chocolate and add toppings to make a special cocoa surprise," she said.

Fatima nodded. "We can use ice to cool it," she said.

"Then the toppings won't melt," added Finn.

"That's a great idea!" said Rosa.

Mr. Darwin handed out ice cubes. Everyone dropped ice into their hot chocolate and waited for it to cool.

"Now for the toppings!"
Libby said.

Rosa used tons
of sprinkles.

Finn added gummy
bears and cookie
crumbles.

Fatima made a whipped
cream mountain covered
with marshmallows and
chocolate chips.

34

Libby used a little bit of everything.

"This is awesome," Fatima said.

"Welcome to our school!" said Libby.

The special cocoa treats were delicious.
The welcome party was a big success.

Best of all, Libby had
a new friend who loved
science as much as she did!

Libby

LOVES SCIENCE

Make your own tasty treats with the three states of matter

Homemade Ice Pops

Materials

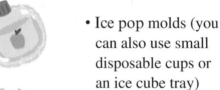

- Your favorite flavor of fruit juice or drink mix

- Wooden craft sticks

- Ice pop molds (you can also use small disposable cups or an ice cube tray)

Instructions

1. Prepare the juice or drink mix according to the instructions on the package.

2. Pour the juice into your ice pop molds, leaving a little space at the top.

3. Insert a craft stick (or toothpick if you're using an ice cube tray). You may need to let the liquid partially freeze in order for the stick to stand up straight.

4. Place the molds in the freezer for several hours or overnight until frozen solid.

5. Once they are fully frozen, remove the ice pops from the freezer and enjoy!

You have turned **juice (a liquid)** into **ice pops (a solid)**.

bubbles!

Homemade Orange Soda

Materials

- Pulp-free orange juice (you can use any citrus juice you like, such as grapefruit, lemon, lime, or orange)

- A glass measuring cup

- Baking soda

- A spoon or straw

Instructions

1. Pour 2/3 of a cup of orange juice into the glass measuring cup. Do not use more than 2/3 of a cup because you will need the space for the carbonation reaction.

2. Add 1 teaspoon of baking soda.

3. Gently stir the baking soda into the juice. It doesn't take long for the orange juice to start to bubble!

The acid in the orange juice (a liquid) reacts with the baking soda (a solid) to create bubbles (a gas) on top. The fizzy, bubbly reaction between the citrus and the baking soda causes "carbonation." Carbon dioxide, a gas, is formed.

Note: This homemade orange soda is safe to drink. Enjoy!

Having fun with **States** of **Matter**
Is It a Solid, Liquid, or Gas?

State of matter?

State of matter?

State of matter?

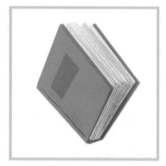

State of matter?

Glossary

Gas: a substance that has no set shape and fills up its entire container. Gases can be invisible!

Liquid: flows freely and takes the shape of its container

Matter: anything that takes up space and has mass

Solid: something that has a definite shape and volume

State: the condition that something is in at a specific time